This edition published by Parragon Books Ltd in 2016

Parragon Books Ltd
Chartist House
15–17 Trim Street
Bath BA1 1HA, UK
www.parragon.com

ISBN 978-1-4748-4284-6

Printed in China

Can't Wait to be Queen

Bath • New York • Cologne • Melbourne • Delhi
Hong Kong • Shenzhen • Singapore

Kiara the lion cub lived with her family in the beautiful African grasslands.

One afternoon, she caught her little brother Kion sharpening his claws on her favourite tree.

"I found it first," she said. "Step aside."
"You can't tell me what to do!" Kion answered.
"Actually, she can," said their dad Simba. "For the next few days, Kiara will be in charge."

Simba explained that he and their mum Nala were going to visit the elephants. "And as Kiara is next in line to the throne, she will be acting queen while we're away," Simba told Kion.

"How long will you be gone?" Kiara asked warily.

"I was nervous about ruling the Pride Lands at first, too," Simba said, "but I have faith in you. Just keep the peace and everything will be fine."

The next morning, Kion and his friends met up at the lions' cave at Pride Rock. They are part of the Lion Guard – a team of fearless and daring animals that protect the kingdom.

Suddenly, Kiara made a grand entrance. "Make way for Her Majesty Queen Kiara!" announced Kiara's friend Zuri.

"She's only queen while Mum and Dad are away," Kion grumbled.

Meanwhile, Mizingo the vulture had flown above Pride Rock and heard everything.

"Hmmm ... Simba and Nala have left their daughter in charge of the Pride Lands. Interesting," he said to himself.

That day, Kiara asked Ono the egret to deliver the Morning Report.

"All is in order," he announced. "The antelope herd is moving along nicely. And I spotted some new beehives nearby."

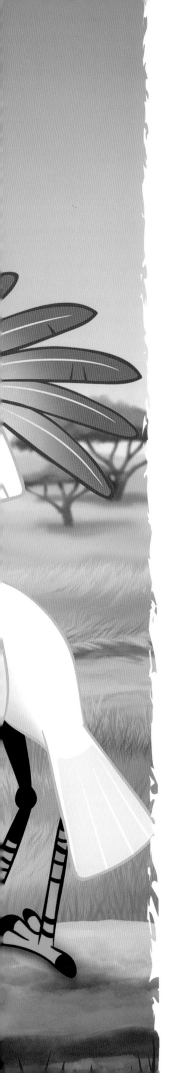

"Wait!" cried Kiara. "The bees might sting the antelope and send the herd into chaos." She turned to her brother. "Kion, you and the Lion Guard must lead the antelope away from the beehives."

Kion rolled his eyes at the Lion Guard.
He thought it was silly to move a whole herd
of antelope just to avoid a few little bees.
"Let's just move the bees," he told his friends.

Kion had been leading the Lion Guard longer than Kiara had been queen, so he wanted to handle things his own way. Besides, what could possibly go wrong?

But everything went wrong!

The Lion Guard made their way back
to Pride Rock, covered in bee stings.
Kiara was not happy. "Maybe next
time you'll listen to your queen. Have you
forgotten that Dad left me in charge?"

Over in the Outlands, Mizingo told Janja the hyena about Kiara and Kion's troubles. "Maybe this is our chance to take over the Pride Lands? I think I have a plan...."

Soon after, Mizingo flew to Pride Rock. He told Kiara that Janja wanted to make peace with the lions. "The hyenas are not welcome in the Pride Lands, so Janja needs you to meet him in the Outlands," squawked Mizingo.

But Kion didn't trust Mizingo or Janja. "It's a trap!" he tried to warn Kiara.

"You just can't stand that I might be right." Kiara said stubbornly. "I am queen, and I'm going!"

Kion stormed off. Just then, his grandfather Mufasa appeared in the clouds and asked Kion why he was upset.

"It's Kiara, Grandfather. She shouldn't believe Janja," Kion explained.

Mufasa wisely told Kion that Kiara would always need her brother's support, especially when she was wrong.

Kion ran as fast as he could back to Pride Rock to find his sister, but she had already left.

"Kiara's in trouble! We have to help her!" he called out to the Lion Guard.

As soon as Kiara arrived at the hyenas' den to talk peace
with Janja, she realized that something was terribly wrong.
"I ... I think I've made a horrible mistake," Kiara whispered.

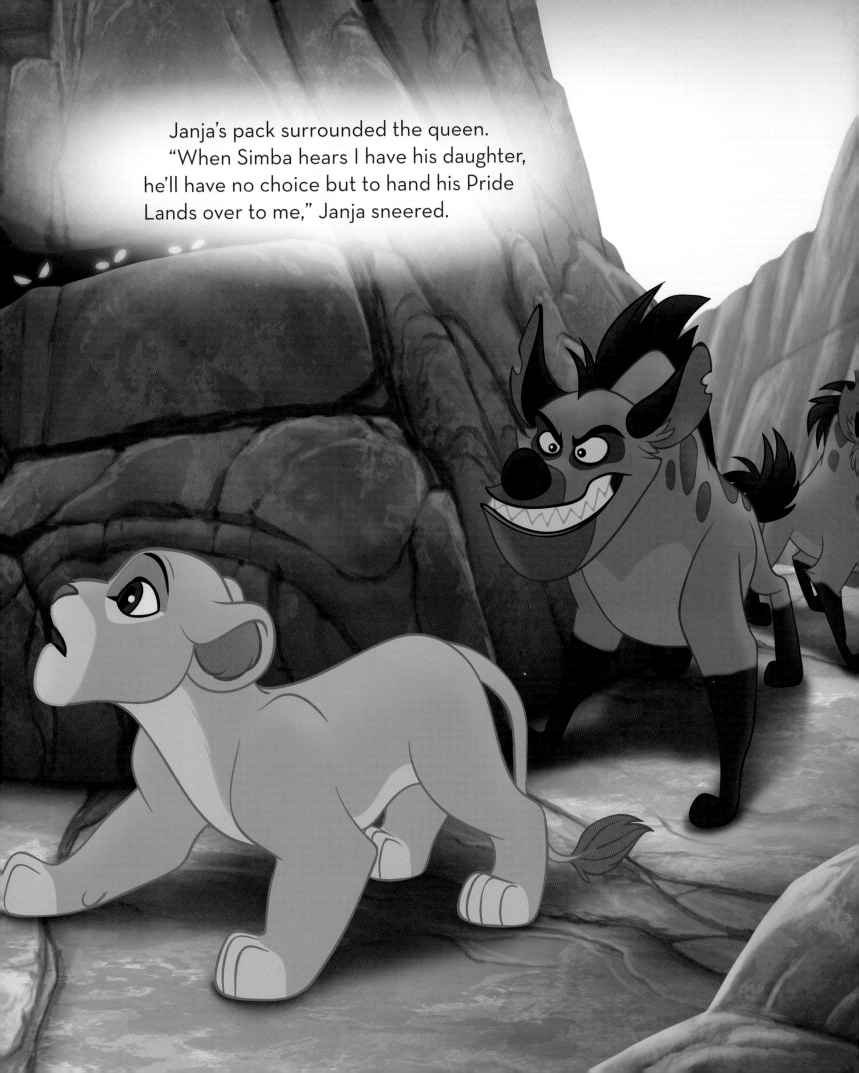

Janja's pack surrounded the queen.
"When Simba hears I have his daughter,
he'll have no choice but to hand his Pride
Lands over to me," Janja sneered.

At that moment, Kion and the Lion Guard leaped into Janja's lair to save Kiara.
"Get away from the queen!" Kion roared.

"Kion, you're here!" Kiara cried.
"Of course!" Kion called back to her.

Janja looked round and realized that the hyenas were surrounded. "Let's get out of here!" he shouted to his pack.

A few days later, Simba and Nala returned.
"Was there any trouble while we were gone?" Simba asked.
"Yes, but nothing Kiara couldn't handle," replied Kion. "She's going to be a great queen ... someday!"

"Thanks for believing in me," Kiara said to her brother.

Kion smiled. "So, I guess you just can't wait to be queen, huh?"

Kiara smiled back. "Maybe I can wait a little longer."